WRITE ACROSS CANADA

Write Across Canada

An Anthology of Emerging Writers

Curated by
Joseph Kertes
&
Geoffrey Taylor

Book*hug Press
Toronto 2019

FIRST EDITION

copyright © 2019 by the authors
introduction copyright © 2019 by Joseph Kertes and Geoffrey Taylor

ALL RIGHTS RESERVED

No part of this publication may be reproduced or transmitted in any form or by any means, electronic or mechanical, including photocopying, recording, or any information storage or retrieval system, without permission in writing from the publisher.

PRINTED IN CANADA

The production of this book was made possible through the generous assistance of the Canada Council for the Arts and the Ontario Arts Council. Book*hug Press also acknowledges the support of the Government of Canada through the Canada Book Fund and the Government of Ontario through the Ontario Book Publishing Tax Credit and the Ontario Book Fund.

Book*hug Press acknowledges that the land on which we operate is the traditional territory of many nations, including the Mississaugas of the Credit, the Anishnabeg, the Chippewa, the Haudenosaunee and the Wendat peoples. We recognize the enduring presence of many diverse First Nations, Inuit and Métis peoples and are grateful for the opportunity to meet and work on this territory.

The image on page 35 and 38 is courtesy of Wikimedia Commons, and was converted to black and white for this publication: https://commons.wikimedia.org/wiki/File:Parrots_Post_Card_UK.jpg

Cover type: Classic Grotesque by Canadian type designer Rod McDonald

TRADE PAPER: 9781771666015
EPUB: 9781771666025
EPDF: 9781771666039
MOBI KINDLE: 9781771666046

Contents

Introduction by Joseph Kertes and Geoffrey Taylor
PAGE 9

British Columbia

Memories from Milk Crates by Miles Steyn
Selected by David Leach
PAGE 13

Conor Kerr: *Granny* by Conor Kerr
Selected by Andrew Gray
PAGE 15

Alberta

Jeannette's Window by Matthew James Weigel
Selected by Thomas Wharton
PAGE 19

Saskatchewan

Invocation by Kate Spencer
Selected by Michael Trussler
PAGE 25

The Car Called Vera by Sarah Mintz
Selected by Michael Trussler
PAGE 26

Manitoba

In Eridu's Blue Light by Matthew Hay
Selected by Jonathan Ball
PAGE 31

Ontario

Afoul of Parliaments by Chloe Burrows Moore
Selected by Karl Jirgens
PAGE 37

2030; A History of Witches by Evelyna Ekoko-Kay
Selected by Catherine Bush
PAGES 41, 43

Moose, Car, Highway; The Cicada Solution by David Dupont
Selected by Michael Helm
PAGES 47, 49

A Brief List of Regrets by Laura Goslinski:
Selected by Andrew Westoll
PAGE 50

(March 18) by Natalia Orasanin
Selected by Dale Smith
PAGE 53

Untitled Excerpt by Colin Buchanan
Selected by David Bezmozgis
PAGE 54

Lighthouse by Aayushi Jain
Selected by Nadia Bozak and Richard Taylor
PAGE 58

Quebec

ELECTRICALS USED & NEW. YOUR APPLIANCES FOR CASH. IN SHOP REPAIRS. by Lars Horn
Selected by Kate Sterns
PAGE 65

New Brunswick

The Country Vet by Charlie Fiset
Selected by Mark Anthony Jarman
PAGE 69

Prince Edward Island

Oy Gevalt; *Cattle Lists*; *My Ravine* by Kandace Hagen
Selected by Richard Lemm
PAGES 75, 77, 79

Nova Scotia

Also Like Life by Ryan Paterson
Selected by Alexander MacLeod
PAGE 83

Life and Limb by Beth Hitchcock
Selected by Kim Pittaway
PAGE 87

Newfoundland

Woolly Adelgid by Amy Donovan
Selected by Robert Finley
PAGE 93

Introduction

What better way to celebrate the 40th anniversary of the Toronto International Festival of Authors than to invite a new wave of thinkers and writers from across the country to contribute stories and poems to this anthology?

Festivals, led by TIFA, have given rise to a national community of readers, helping to spawn a national community of writers with uniquely Canadian perspectives and uniquely diverse voices. These voices represent a broad range of cultures and experiences, including previously underrepresented voices from Indigenous communities, immigrants, refugees, and the LGBTQ2S+ community.

Over the years, TIFA and similar festivals have encouraged writers and given them a platform to share their work. Publishers continue to embrace these voices and share them with readers around the world. University and college writing programs have sprouted up in all ten provinces and in the territories, in addition to writing organizations, writing circles, and community book clubs.

The fiction, non-fiction, and poetry in this anthology, selected by creative writing mentors from across the country, represent a mere sampling of work by emerging writers in Canada today. These writers are fresh voices on their way to becoming seasoned artists and perhaps even some of them, household names or international stars. They are worthy heirs to the Festival, begun 40 years ago, which continues to bring together writers from across Canada and around the world.

Joseph Kertes and Geoffrey Taylor
October 2019

British Columbia

Memories from Milk Crates
Miles Steyn

When I think of mangoes I think of my father who thinks of my sister when he thinks of mangoes. It is hard to think of anything else in Durban, South Africa, where teens sell Kents and Zills and Titan Tommies from milk crates on the highway shoulder and at every exit.

In summer, the humidity can ripen mangoes in an afternoon. Neglected on the kitchen counter, they rot by morning. And so, when Taylor and I were young, Dad would buy only one mango at a time and return before breakfast to boast about his find, a specimen so heavy it must have dropped from the tree by itself. There was always no mango bigger or sweeter in the world—proof, he'd claim, that Africa is the Cradle of Humankind and Everything Else.

Then he'd leave us to monitor his latest pick. We would watch it blush and freckle under the veranda's shade, and fetch him once we'd declared it ready. We stepped into bathing suits still cool from yesterday's swim and prepared our backyard pool for the Eucharist, using the netted skimmer like a thurible to cleanse the water of sunken leaves and drowned dragonflies. Dad would anoint our noses with zinc and consecrate the mango in a chlorine bath.

He was dexterous with his knife. He'd carve the skin from the flesh, snatch the first leathery strap with his teeth, let Taylor take the second piece balanced between his thumb and the blade, and then measure an equal cut for me. One for him, one for her, one for me. We'd follow that order down to the hairy pip, which Dad would then hurl into the deep end and race us for the last few resinous licks.

I'd keep my head down and kick like hell in the direction I thought it landed. Often, by the time I came up for air and rubbed the sting from my eyes to search for what was already gone, Taylor would be seated on the lip of the deep end, juice slipping down her wrists.

I was consoled by the fact of tomorrow: there would be another race, another mango.

Tomorrow came and then it didn't. We immigrated to Canada and settled in a tiny townhouse on the hem of East Vancouver, where the three of us shared the occasional mango over the kitchen sink.

Tomorrow came and then it disappeared altogether. Taylor died making a left turn onto the road that would have brought her home, and Dad hasn't browsed a produce aisle since.

When I think of mangoes I think of my father who thinks of my sister when he thinks of mangoes. Last summer I could think of nothing else when we returned to Durban without Taylor for the first time, drove by the teens selling Kents and Zills and Titan Tommies on the roadside.

But Dad didn't pull over to sort through the waxy pyramids for a mango with deceptive heft and a slight rise at its stem and a little give under his palm and skin that wrinkled at the pressure of his thumb because he believed every touch could alter it irrevocably—another scratch, another bruise, each time drawing further from the perfect fruit.

He moved on, switched lanes, put the teens selling memories from milk crates in his rear-view mirror. He said the mangoes would be sweeter next month. He said we'd never finish one, just the two of us. He said fine, that maybe we could try tomorrow.

Granny
Connor Kerr

"I hear you, my boy." My grandmother's face is in every notokesiw that sits outside the liquor stores that run up and down Whyte Avenue. Her laugh is in every ask for spare change from the mooniyaw walking past her. Her bones and blood are in every blade of grass, every leaf and needle, every speck of dirt, every drop of rain. Her voice is in the mufflers of the motorcycles and the laughter of the drunk university students. Her footsteps shuffle back and forth across the land where her ancestors were born. The concrete boxes of bars, restaurants, pawn shops, liquor stores, clothing stores, cheap trinket stores, and vintage stores where she ended up.

She got her news from eavesdropping on the conversations of smokers and people drinking beer on patios. She had become invisible to their eyes, and they stared right through her. When she didn't understand their words, she used her imagination to fill in the blanks. To her, there was no difference between the importance of national politics and teen-girl drama. I would sit beside her on the bench outside the karaoke lounge, chain-smoking borrowed cigarettes and talking.

"Did you hear that Andrew and Megan hooked up last night and she forgot her boyfriend's hoodie in Andrew's room?"

"Namoya, Granny. Not that one."

"What about Obama being a Jew?"

"What?"

"Pfft. You're out of it, my boy."

When they were young, her sisters would get her to buy the booze. "You're the white one," they'd chant in unison, "you don't get in any trouble." And she'd put on her reddest lipstick, a fake wedding ring, and her nicest dress to wander over to the liquor store and pick up some cheap wine. Her mother often said to her, "You're lucky. You can pass. Your sisters, now, they're in trouble."

She needed the drink to stop the shake. She shook so bad she could no longer place the tiny red, blue, and white beads on her needle without it. The drop-in centre said No Booze, Drugs, or Weapons on the door, but she needed a nip to be able to bead. And the old man who ran the program didn't care. That sign was for the young people, or the ones who screamed in voices, not the old ladies from the avenue.

In the summers she slept behind the old brick public library building or under the Mill Creek bridge. She had this big old blanket, red faded to orange, with a bison skull on it. The blanket never left her side, and even when she was asking for change she'd use it to cover her lap properly. She told me that when she died I should throw her in the river, because she wanted to see her cousin, who had moved to Prince Albert, one last time. The other day a young woman shuffled by me with the blanket on her shoulders. I thought I heard her whisper, "I hear you, my boy."

Alberta

Jeannette's Window
Matthew James Weigel

When the ship that carried Jeannette Villepreux-Power's collections, records, and equipment sank off the coast of France in 1848, her lifework was returned to the sea. From that time on, she no longer engaged in scientific research.

I invented the aquarium in 1832.

It was just a small box made of glass, but when I poured in ocean water and it caught the sun, my heart was filled with light. Before the water brought this magic, air alone had transmitted these rays and the light accentuated the box's emptiness. Water caught the rays and bounced them throughout the room. I was uplifted by a liquid beauty, a little glowing box of water. A ripple of the water's shadow moved across my dress as though I were in the throes of dance while standing still. Compelled by the joy of light and ocean that I felt within me, I took up this signal, and my feet and body moved in dance.

My youth was far away, and I thought over my journey. Home was the greenery of Juillac and its cool-water creeks, where I would rest my feet on warm afternoons. I had spent so many cheerful days in exploration, turning over rocks to look for hidden creatures, searching the fresh and flowing streams for pearl-bearing mussels. I was eighteen when I left Juillac and walked the 450 kilometres to Paris. Juillac's trees and gorges were so different from the tall buildings and narrow streets of the capital, but the complexities of society life interested me in the same manner as the forest. In Paris, I made dresses, embroidering with pearls that caught the light as the ladies danced. My skills caught attentions, and I was tasked with producing the wedding gown of Princess Caroline. Greater attentions gathered, and soon after, James and I were married and making a new home for ourselves in Sicily.

There I felt an overflowing of love for the sparkling ocean, and longed to experience it more fully. This shore held long-limbed scarlet sea stars, pink sponges, and flitting fish of orange and blue. My fascination with mussels and how they formed their pearls was amplified at the sight of the elegant spiral case of the argonaut. This clever octopus carried a secret in its shell, and I was drawn to investigate. The aquarium let me set foot beneath the sea without taking a single step.

All the stages of a life are a wonder. Our entire path contributes to our development. When I stood in front of that first aquarium, I was struck with this notion, that I was precisely where I needed to be. I felt illuminated, like some specimen beneath a microscope, and I saw myself and the path that put me there. This new device allowed me to see all the stages of the argonaut's life, how its delicate shell progressed from a grain's weight to its adult size. In this discovery, I formed my life of science.

The aquarium's waterlight sent vibrations in a tingle through my extremities. A warmth filled my core. My ears burned. The roots of my hair shivered in a path along my scalp, down my neck, and around my sides to curl in turbulence within my belly. The luminosity of the natural world felt expansive, felt as great as the sea. Warmed by this light, I wondered if this may have been as Newton felt, as Galileo felt. The glass of my aquarium, through which I was the first to see the argonaut construct its shell, was like the prism that splits the sunlight to show us the colours of its composition. Or the fine lenses that brought the moons of Jupiter within our view.

It was not just a small box made of glass: it was a window.

I saw inside the sea and in the rivers of Sicily. I saw how these taxed rivers could be made whole again. If I could rear the paper nautilus for research, what might local industry do for native fish and crustaceans? The warmth I felt became a cooling shiver when I thought upon what good might be accomplished through my invention.

I corresponded regularly with all the European academies on these subjects, as there is a considerable demand for knowledge. At London I saw the Regent's Park fish house, earliest of the public displays now common throughout the continent. I am overjoyed to see such oceanic passions in the public brought about by the practice. Indeed, it is now quite fashionable for aquariums to be kept in the home, and much trade has developed in support of this habit.

But the fashions of London and Paris appeared much smaller to me since my world became the sea. The streets were not the crowded rock pools of searching fish and scuttling hermit crabs. The parks were not the shore.

James and I abandoned Paris when we received word of the approaching Prussian army. With little hesitation I knew my path was finally bringing me home. Not to Sicily, where I knew the sea would be unbearable in its reminder of my losses, but to Juillac.

It is winter. I recall those hot Sicilian days and expansive thoughts of future study, but these recollections bring a sadness. I may still write and speak of science, but I no longer pursue those broader thoughts. A winter in the hills will suit, and spring is always so exquisite here, a lovely green cut through by cooling streams. Out the window now it is cloudy, and I see only falling snow through a hazy light. The cold tightens the skin of my face. My body feels small and heavy. But soon the frost will be melted, and the light will warm again.

That January in 1871, Jeannette died in Juillac, France.

Saskatchewan

Invocation
Kate Spencer

you are missing
from my first bedroom—
yellow, bright beside shaky

and ancient train tracks. you are missing,
vanished from the sunny pantry,
vanilla and sugar cubes left unattended.

you are missing. from each recipe
card i try to conjure your laugh,
but you are missing still.

from photos—the first christmas
after the hospital, and all our April
birthdays—you are missing.

from the cedar-lined chest
still soaked in your smell, half-
full of our things, you are

missing. the letters signed
your name, now strange

syllables in black ink.

The Car Called Vera
Sarah Mintz

My grandmother kept a razor in her car when I was a kid. She would shave spots she missed on her legs because she couldn't see in the low light of the bathroom. It never seemed weird or gross but to say it out loud it does. Her car always seemed beachy and peaceful and faded and crisped by the sun. Somehow the razor fit right in with the beach blankets and beach toys. She doesn't keep a razor in her car anymore. She's got a Vibe now and it doesn't feel open and summery and it doesn't smell like dried seawater or driftwood. It's a zippy little red car that reminds me of her sister because her sister has red hair and always used to drive a red car. I think maybe my grandmother got a red car because she would have thought that she shouldn't because her sister's cars were always red, then she would have resisted the idea that she shouldn't and played ignorant if anyone dared to bring it up. Of course, no one ever would. But her car doesn't smell like the beach anymore. It smells a bit like a hospital, an industrial hospital. Like the smell of the place they make wheelchairs. Wherever that is and whatever that smells like. Probably it's because of her variety of canes and walking aids with neat features, and orthopedic shoes. All the things she keeps in her car to enable her decaying state to continue to walk and drive—though everyone wants her to stop—to maintain her freedom. But whether or not we take it away or the encroaching smell of a hospital displaces the smell of the beach, it's fading. Her freedom is fading because her body is dying, her mind is dying, and her time is dying. But she wants it still. I want it, too. For me, already noticing that things don't have the same shape they used to. My face, my body, my feet, harder, more callused, nails less curved, skin less elastic, all things just conspiring to one day hold me down. And for her. I want her to keep her accumulated knowledge; I don't want to have to squeeze it out of her in an effort to save memories, memories no one will ever again see or know or hear or feel. I want her to keep them. I want the living embodiment of those memories to keep them and keep her body and keep growing until she's everywhere bigger than everything and we have all her memories still, and maybe—anyway, maybe that is what happens. Maybe the stories that never get told get to be known anyway. No matter how stupid they are.

Manitoba

In Eridu's Blue Light
Matthew Hay

Micah leaned against the smooth railing of his balcony and thought that he did not deserve paradise. Victoria, his newly assigned life partner, looked out also, with a smile.

From up here they could see all of Eridu, spread out before them like a platter of ripe fruit. An orb of blue fire soared out from the centre of the city, up past pristine skyscrapers that crowded around to watch. It streaked high into the violet atmosphere, but before the stars could assimilate it, the luminous orb exploded outward in a radiant supernova.

Victoria laughed aloud.

Micah frowned.

The brightness of the blue light could not wash out the memory of his brother, Vance, handing over his final application forms for Eridu. *Be careful with these, please.* He pushed the envelope into Micah's hands before rushing out the door. *It has to be in today, Micah!* Vance was always on the move. Micah had held the papers with trembling fingers.

Closing his eyes now, Micah willed the memory dampeners he'd taken this morning to come into effect and douse the image of his brother's trusting smile with buckets of apathy. But the drugs were slow-acting, and his memories still smouldered.

"Incredible!" Victoria said, still looking to the sky.

"Hmm."

She turned away to look at him, and her smile faltered. Then returned, but forced this time. "Let's go inside and finish the wine."

Micah didn't respond, but he let Victoria lead him through the sliding door and into their new, luxurious apartment. He turned his head to look back past the balcony to the sky, where a series of smaller blue orbs rocketed into the air. They also exploded, silently.

She went into the kitchen, while he took a seat in the living room, leaving room for her on the leather couch.

"Do you want a glass?"

"No," he said.

She returned with two wineglasses anyway and poured two drinks, but sat on the other couch. "Try it, please. It's probably not what you're used to up in the Fords, but it's the best we had at my family's pub."

Micah took a sip, regretting the bitter liquid as it flowed down his tongue. With a quick swallow, he set the glass down.

"Do you believe in this place?" she asked after taking a long sip.

"My father does, told us it's an escape—"

"From what?" She shook her head. "I escaped. Would've given anything to live up in the Fords, never mind Eridu."

"The Fords was no paradise."

"Clean water, private education, security, medicine..." She took a great gulp of wine. "A lot closer to paradise, at least."

Nipping at his drink, he stayed quiet for a long moment.

When Vance had been selected by their father to go to Eridu, Micah wasn't surprised. No one had ever thought Micah would go—especially not Micah. Not until Vance handed him the manila envelope did Micah's mind hum with the possibility. It would be easy to change just a few key things on Vance's forms, disqualify him. Until that moment, Micah had never considered how easily one could succeed, could change everything.

"Well, you're here now," he said, the memory fading.

"True."

Micah frowned. "Did you think you were going to get into Eridu?"

She gave him a queer look, said, "Let's not talk about who

we used to be. Doesn't matter anyhow. Those drugs will wipe away our memories tonight—"

"Dampen," he corrected her. "The memory dampeners *dampen* our memories, make us stop caring about them. But we'll still have them, we just won't care."

This seemed to throw her, and she stared into her drink. "Sounds worse."

Micah remembered Vance stepping into his room. Vance's eyes dark, a few tears running down his face. Micah took a long sip of his wine. "No."

She frowned, then looked toward the balcony. "I need to see those lights again."

"Okay."

Following her out onto the balcony, Micah felt a tremor emanate from somewhere deep below the building. "Do you feel that?" he asked, gripping the balcony's railing. "Maybe we should go back inside."

"Embrace it."

He shivered.

Before them, another light, larger than all the others, flew out of the city's core like an asteroid going the wrong way.

It kept rising, that blue light, like some new sun.

The urge to weep overcame him. A few tears streaked his face and he brushed them away with his thousand-dollar sleeve. He imagined his brother standing beside him on the balcony. *I misjudged you,* Vance said, eyes steady on Micah's face. *But I won't tell anyone. I can't take Eridu from you.* Vance got onto the railing. *But there's nothing for me here, not now.*

Then he leaned forward and dropped off the edge.

Micah shut his eyes.

He escaped the balcony, sought relief in the bedroom. A few minutes later, Victoria appeared in the open doorway, staring down to where he sat on the bed.

Neither said a word as she slipped out of her dress. Micah

stared up at the ceiling, leaving ample room for her on the bed—this time she moved into the space he had left, although she waited a long moment to do so. Then she moved overtop of him, hovering, kissing his face with listless lips. Eyes shut, he did his best to mimic the way her lips moved. He fumbled off his pants, his body cold and unstirred.

For a short while they pantomimed lovers he'd only seen on glowing screens, but nothing came of it. With a dry kiss on his tear-stained cheek, she left him for her side of the bed.

With a sigh, he turned away from her as well.

He lay awake all night, stomach churning with dread. Only in the morning did the dampeners finally take effect, soothing his anxiety while the rising sun turned a lifetime of memories to stone.

Ontario

Afoul of Parliaments
Chloe Burrows Moore

The time finally came when the birds had had enough at the city zoo. The Parrots wanted to plan a revolution. Break free of their enclosure. Escape the monotony of pressed faces and pointing fingers. Two wings good. Two legs bad.

They assembled a Parliament of Fowls, not to choose their mate, but rather their fate. They readied for debate, and waited for the right words.

Ah, the curse of Echo. To wait for someone to speak. *Please, anything but "Polly want a cracker?"*

They squawked loudly, grasping at sounds, phonemes, words they could not pronounce.

"Look, Mommy! Pretty birds!" a boy child shrieked from *out there.*

The King of the Parrots called their attention: "Look, birds!"

The chatter quieted down. The birds ruffled their feathers and took their places upon the branches acting as benches for their assembly.

"Polly want a cracker?" a human cooed.

"Want," the King said.

"Here, birdie birdie. Here, birdie birdie."

"Hear, hear," the assembly of birds cried out.

Then the humans moved on, and the birds waited.

"Hear, hear," a small bird said again.

They continued to wait. The sounds of other animals, entirely useless to them, filled the silence. Bees buzzed. Geese honked. A monkey screeched in the distance.

A few of the young birds eyed some popcorn the child had dropped on the pavement outside. Finally, two people approached.

"Hey, look. Are these the ones that talk?" a passing human called to a friend.

"Look. Talk," the King asserted.

"Oh, neat," the human said. He let out a string of profanities, hoping the birds would catch on.

The King swore in frustration.

The humans moved on, and then the next few passersby uttered more nonsense. Nothing worth repeating. The humans talked and taunted them but grew increasingly dissatisfied when the birds refused to mimic them.

"This is useless. Let's get out of here."

"This is useless. Let's get out of here," the King suggested.

The assembled birds ruffled their feathers at the suggestion. They looked to one another. Could they really leave?

A child squealed in delight. "But he talked! Let's not go yet!" She laced her fingers into the looped wire of the cage, rattling it. "Speak!"

"But," a young bird said. "Let's talk. Let's not go. Let's speak."

The child's mother shushed her. She knelt down beside her daughter. "If we lower our voices, we can stay. We need to be quiet, or we'll scare them. Then we'll have to leave."

The little girl nodded with her finger to her lips. In a loud whisper she said, "I want to stay and talk to the birds."

The young bird took a deep breath. "If we leave, we have to be quiet. We will lower our voices. We can stay. Stay and talk."

"Mommy, why are they caged?" the girl asked.

The King protested, "Why caged?"

"So they don't fly away," the mother said.

"Fly away," the King said.

"Why would they fly away?" The little girl pressed her nose through the links of the fence. She could almost reach the blue feathers of a female macaw sitting on the branch. "They have toys and food and nice little perches. If I was a bird, I'd like a nice place like this to live."

The young bird spread his wings wide. "Why fly away?" he asked. "Toys. Food. Nice perches. Nice place to live. Why fly away?"

The King looked to the little girl and her mother in desperation. *Please, say something worth repeating. Please help me. Say that birds are meant to fly. Say that birds need to be free, not caged.*

The mother shrugged. "That's just the way animals are."

The King rearranged the words in his head. "That's the way are," he tried.

The birds cocked their heads in confusion.

He tried again, "Animals. The way." He gestured to the sky with his wing.

"It's a nice home," the girl reasserted.

"It's a nice home," the young bird said.

No! We are prisoners! the King wanted to scream. *We must leave!* But the words he wanted would not come.

"It's a nice home," another bird agreed.

"It's a nice home," the parliament said in unison.

Not home! We must roam! We must roam.

But the assembly was over. The decision made. The birds

dispersed. Flew to their own spaces in the enclosure: a branch, a perch, a little hammock. The young bird nipped at a juicy pineapple ring left by the zookeepers.

"Stay, birdie, stay," the girl said, stepping back from the cage.

"Stay, stay, stay," they squawked.

"Pretty birds," the little girl said as she turned and walked away.

The King bird preened his feathers. There was nothing he could say to that.

Two Poems
Evelyna Ekoko-Kay

2030

you call me at 1:43 a.m. and say we're all gonna fucking die
we can't kill a few fucking billionaires so we're all gonna die
it snowed early this november and I lost my voice
I think about us all that night lying on the floor in stacks
between your boyfriend's couches and the bedroom door
us at the protest with my right eye cracking in the heat
you in your red skirt playing medic. we can't sleep at night
we paint our molars green. kneel our faces in the washroom sink
I can't help you when you vomit in a metro bag but I'll be waiting
in the kitchen with a cup of rice on the bottom left burner

we're all gonna fucking die I say and go to second cup
we're all gonna fucking die I say and hand you a bandana
on the stove the rice is boiling over. you're on the counter
with your mouth between your knees I don't know how to
stop this. I practise crying in a mirror but my face still melts
there are things I won't do and for that we're going to die
we haven't talked much lately. I see your shoulders on ctv
I walk outside at 4:00 p.m. in my pyjamas and say to a squirrel
I am a communist and the squirrel doesn't answer. it's okay
I put a rock between my teeth and bite. we've got 12 years
so I pack a bowl and leave the stove on cut my hair again

there are things I won't do. we're all gonna fucking die
you say I say we're all gonna fucking die you say yeah
I'm scared to cut an avocado. I haven't seen a dentist
in two years. it's 5:00 p.m. so it's okay to drink a glass of wine
I want to call you tell you stay the night I'll be a flat of salt

I'll be your shadow's shadow I'll put the left half of my tongue
inside a box. last week I saw you standing in st lawrence west
talking about global warming with a bag of rice between your legs
I don't stop walking. I think of that bedroom in your mother's house
where I drew portraits on the floor by the mirror. some of us will die
you said. I want to spend the rest of my life here with this sketch pad,
these pencil crayons. some of us will live I say and turn the stove off

A History of Witches

1982.
my mother skipped school so often in yaounde
that even her light skin
could not save her.
expelled into a home with a tin roof
which her sisters called the hole
she read the magic carpet
eight times down at the american club
before trying to bewitch
the kitchen rug   or the chair   or the closet where
her father hung his suits   from england.

she used to find pieces of her mamma's hair
under the insole of her daddy's shoe.
she'd steal the hair
and throw it in the ocean by the cove.
he was a man with a mean step her daddy
used to jingle car keys in his pocket
though he didn't own a car
told the village men of his brother
the magistrate   told his daughters
"don't walk by the water in the dark"
asked them, spit like seafoam on his lips
"are you sluts? are you all little sluts?"
once, when the sun was heavy on the sky
he left   and came back two days later
with a dead porcupine   which he cooked
and made them eat
with their rice and beans.
you can't trust a man like that with magic.

1986.
every good tailor is a witch.
when things got bad
my mother's mother started working
dark hours at her shop in town.
there's no accounting for it really
one day they were   as poor as an unmarked grave
the next she had   four women to do the stitching
and a government car
with a soldier in the driver's seat.
the women of my family have a knack
for getting the world
for the cost of thread.
bought their way out of cameroon   and landed in toronto
with just an address in my mother's pocket.

1989.
in the third-floor bedroom
of that house on hughson street
there was a dream with clenching hands
which held my mother's head
underwater every night   until she drowned.
there were three women in that room
my mother, auntie rosa, and their mother
who lay her futon by the pedal of the
sewing machine and told them
"there is nothing here   go back to sleep."
my mother and my auntie
started sleeping in the living room
afraid of the weight on their chests
afraid of the hands at their throats.
my mother started sewing

amaranth into their shirts
and keeping scissors by the pillow.
it was only later when they lived
in westdale by the college   that their mother said
"I used to dream it too."

now.
my mother says "I was a witch"
and I believe it.
I want to be like this
like the women who walked
the floor of the atlantic
to love their children in this place of smoke.
who cut their hair at home still by the washroom sink
and bury it in the garden by the black-eyed susans.
I wear all black and spin like a phantom in the hall.
I take the blood from out of me in lines.
I write a letter to my granddaddy
and lock it in a drawer.

at last, my mother sits me at the table
and says "girl, stop all this weeping."
says "we didn't cross seas
dance knives   swallow language
till it turned dark and bloody like a sacrifice
for you to seek the monsters we have buried."
says "you do not have this
kind of magic in your veins."
says "that is a good thing.
you do not want the kind of life
that makes a girl a witch."

"I love you" she says
"because you are going to
grow up tall   never catching
quills in your teeth
or a needle in your finger."

Moose, Car, Highway
David Dupont

The great bull lowered his heavy head, his antlers laden with snow, and stood his ground against the two bright white shapes that grew steadily closer. He thought of the flying pests that nagged him during summer, how with a shake he could find momentary relief, and he shook; but the white shapes held their course. A challenge. He snorted exhaust in the deep freeze of the dropping wind chill. With the wind came a drone, a wind on *top* of the wind, also growing in intensity. And with it the smell, not piss or food or shit or musk, but a caustic river of pollution that coated his lungs. He found all of it offensive. After three days of marching through knee-high banks, he was sore, and grateful to be on this plowed stretch of highway under the cold bright moonlight—he would not give it up easily.

A thick snow fell and made it harder for him to see. He focused, his eye busting out of his skull like a sunken eight ball, down the long road until he once again spotted the white shapes, bigger now than the falling snowflakes, easier to follow. Soon he was unable to look away, and his senses roasted his insides. The fire burning in his belly fevered him. He struggled against hypnosis, and was confused and angry. His ears lay back and the hair on his neck bristled while he clicked his teeth. With his left foreleg he stomped, hammering out danger.

He stepped closer, slowly at first but soon picking up speed, until he was trotting toward the brightness. A sudden sustained note blasted across the night air and punished his eardrums, for an instant distracting him from his footing, but now he was unstoppable. As the white closed in, the bull's consciousness flooded with images long forgotten, forgotten once again as soon as they passed: a calf, trapped in snow;

plentiful food; fucking; a duel; a cedar, browning at its edges; a shallow river cold on his ankles as he crosses; more, now gone, flushed away by the oncoming light as he charged forward.

The Cicada Solution
David Dupont

Auntie Nora had brought the whole business on herself, as far as I was concerned, with those ridiculous teeth of hers. The upper plate roamed, clicking and clacking. It was probably that sound—underscored by the lisp of a story I'd heard three times since the amuse-bouche—that had stirred to a frenzy the insects surrounding the courtyard of Le Bistro Fontaine. She had just managed enough suction to open wide and gulp down a breath when a cicada sprang from the bushes and into her mouth. I watched it grip her uvula and strangle her from the inside.

I couldn't risk having the waiter see her choke. He'd already delivered the bill and was looming, so I sent him away to boil a fresh pot of Auntie Nora's favourite tea. Not much time. But I would expect that at ninety-five she'd be quick about it.

Her face turned such a bruised blue I had no choice but to look away. I closed my eyes and thought of Nice. There were sizzling shores, and hotel staff who knew me by name. Never again would I wait for a table. I would race along the coast in a sports car, although I knew nothing of sports cars. The slightest of hoods forming above my eyes would be addressed, and my hands would be done regularly, and my feet. Even at eighteenth in line there was plenty enough to go around. The family better thank me for this.

I was finishing her lemon water, lest she get any ideas about washing it down, when Auntie Nora suddenly managed such a spluttering hack that I was certain she was trying to dislodge the assailant with chatter. Her eyes popped, and from her throat she spit the bug onto the table. Its wings were soggy. It tightened its head. It looked weak, and measly. Such a large specimen; such an anticlimax. I trapped it beneath my empty glass.

Auntie Nora clung to her chest through layers of pearls.

Eye contact would be impossible.

A Brief List of Regrets
Laura Goslinski

If you hadn't taken his hand at four o'clock in the morning, as the shallow beat of house music shook the porch boards, you wouldn't have woken up to the honking of Mrs. Morts on her morning drive to Tims. You are wearing the short blue sequined dress you wore the night before to that party you didn't want to go to and are having a hard time remembering, but you're also zipped into a gigantic name-brand parka. The parka is big enough to swim in, but it doesn't go past your knees, so your calves and ankles and bare feet are turning purple. Whoever gave you the parka didn't think about how cold your feet would be when you woke up to Mrs. Morts getting out of her car to see you lying in the middle of the road, snow shoved away from your outstretched arms, your gigantic parka and chilly toes laid atop an impressed snow angel.

"What are you doing out here? Do your parents know you're here? Of course they don't. I'm going to call your mother. She must be worried. Oh, your toes, look at your toes." Her arms are tucked under her armpits, a phone pressed to her red cheek. You can hear your mother's muffled voice. All the while the only thing you can think is how cold your hands are and how Mrs. Morts isn't getting you a blanket, so instead you let your eyes roll to the heavy grey sky.

"Your mother is on her way." But you can hear the snow rumbling, so that takes your attention. She blows a fogged breath through her nose. "I suppose whoever was out here with you took off. How irresponsible of them to not make sure you were following." You look to your right, where a snow angel has been.

If you hadn't taken that tab he gave you at two o'clock in the morning, as a girl was hurling Denny's into the sink at that party you're starting to remember, you never would have taken his hand at four o'clock in the morning. The walls were changing colour, and your tongue was the size of an apartment building, but he said it was quieter outside. That didn't make sense to you because it was perfectly quiet among the bouncing bodies and bumping beers; all you could feel was the wave pool under the floorboards, and all you could hear was his voice. Fingers pulsing between his, you found your way to the front porch. Snow crunched beneath your toes, heat radiating up your leg.

"Come look at this," he said, and he led you down the steps and into the middle of the road. It was always quiet at that time of night. The trees lining the road whispered welcomes as you reached the spot where a seam sewed up the space. "Remember what happened here?"

You looked at the ground, where the two pavements met, and looked back up at him. "I think the world's gonna split in half."

"It's not gonna split in half. Don't worry." He held your shoulders, and his forehead creased the way it always did when he was worried. It made his eyebrows poke out.

"No, no, I feel like it's going to rip in half, and you've brought me here because this is where it's gonna happen because this is where the world is glued together."

He smiled, dropping his hands. "How is it glued together?"

"Hot glue. The world maker went to Michaels and bought them all out, but hot glue isn't that strong when it gets wet, and it's wet everywhere."

"It's frozen wet, the hot glue will hold a moment longer, it has to melt, don't worry. We have time." Then he pulled off his jacket and wrapped it around your shoulders. "And if the world does split in half, this will protect you." Then he drew you to the ground, and you lay beside him and listened to the world makers. Sometimes they would tell you to look at him because there wouldn't be many moments left to look at him, so you would, and he would already be looking at you like they had said the same thing to him. When you could feel the frozen wet begin to melt, he said, "You know, it's going to be okay."

"I don't want it to." You squeezed your eyes shut and pressed your palms into the pavement. Suddenly everything was too bright, and you could feel the snow nipping your palms, and you could smell his dollar-store cologne on the parka. "The world's splitting in half, all the houses are falling into the middle."

"I'll call you."

"All the phones fell in, too."

"I'll email you."

"The internet tubes are gone, eaten by the broken."

He turned over onto his side and put a wet hand on your cheek. "Look at me."

You opened your eyes; there were spots, and a darkness around the edges. He looked at you the same way he did when you kissed for the first time, many snows ago, feet planted firmly on either side of this same seam.

"I'm here," he said.

"Don't say that."

"Let me walk you home."

"I want to be here when it happens."

If you hadn't taken his hand at ten o'clock a long time ago, and kissed him at this seam, you wouldn't have gone to the party where you wanted to forget, and you wouldn't have taken his hand at four o'clock, and you wouldn't have fallen asleep, and he wouldn't have slipped away. If none of that had happened, you wouldn't have to look at your mom now as she wraps you in a blanket with that look, the look that says heartbreak is a sinkhole in a perfectly paved road.

(March 18)
Natalia Orasanin

there is a room I cannot touch
when the worms are out
the squirrels reside in a place where the river
bends meeting the path to the mountaintop
pebbles press the soles of my feet—
legs aching toward an oven light
right here
where the tree gave me a scar the shape of a robin
I get lost in the middle all over again
I put the twig from behind the fence
under my pillow
to remember the way
I scraped my knee picking
pieces of grass to wrap
my chestnut offering
gift gone in the morning
my friend will never come back
I scream reaching the mountaintop
to make my mother laugh

Untitled Excerpt
Colin Buchanan

"Jake thinks Mom set him up," said Shelley.

Those six words hung in the air—for Tim at the pay phone on Cloud Four, as the patients called their unit in CAMH, and for Shelley in her dad's kitchen. Tim could almost feel Shelley shaking through the telephone line.

"Okay, don't freak out, Shel. Where's Mom?"

"She went to stay with that lawyer she's been seeing, someplace downtown."

"Oh, cool, a lawyer might come in handy in the near future."

"He's a fucking *real estate* lawyer, Tim. He doesn't go for no big courtroom dramas."

"Well, but she's safe there, right?"

"No worse than anyplace else, I wouldn't imagine." Shelley sounded tired. "She told me Jake is drunk and on painkillers all the time. The basement is a big fucking mess. He won't clean it up. No way anybody can come look at the house if they want to buy it."

"You just stay cool, okay, and if that fucker shows up at your place, call the cops right away. I'll figure out something to do. Just relax, Shel, okay? Tell Mom to call me."

"Alright. Let me know what's going on."

"You too, Shel. Love you."

As he hung up, he tried to remember the last time he'd told Shelley he loved her. Wouldn't come to him.

Tim was pacing the hallway by the cafeteria when he spotted Ezekiel, motionless and barely visible against a wall, pipe in his mouth, his head erect, with the bearing of an army general.

"Ezekiel, I know you don't like to talk, but I have to ask you something. You're a peace-loving man, right?"

Ezekiel took a half step away from the wall, put his pipe in his bathrobe pocket, his arms behind his back, and said stentoriously, "Yes."

"I thought so. But what about, in certain situations, like

protecting your family, say...are there some times when violence is okay? For the greater good?"

Ezekiel slowly lowered his gaze to Tim's. Did Ezekiel ever blink? He didn't now. He very quietly cleared his throat and said, "Yes." He retrieved his pipe from his pocket, nodded at Tim, gave an upside-down wink, and shuffled silently away.

Esmerelda's fists turned red as Tim told her what was going on. He filled her in on more of the details of what had happened down south, but mostly he told her what Jake had done to Shelley and himself.

"That little thing that's come visiting you? He messed around with her?"

"Yeah. I just found out a little while ago."

"And he beat the shit out of you?"

"Just, yeah, well...actually a lot of times."

Esmerelda opened her fists and began patting her palms on the cafeteria table. She looked out the window at the lunatic's wall, and in the window's reflection she saw Danny coming up. She beckoned him over.

"Up for a mission, Danny-boy? We need to help this guy here." She indicated Tim without looking at him. "He's got one guy fucking up a whole bunch of lives who really oughta be taught some good ol' fashioned Portuguese manners."

Turned out Portuguese manners weren't too different from what could reasonably be regarded as the Golden Rule. Esmerelda explained that her father had come from Portugal, started working construction about ten minutes after he got off the train, and still works it today. Tough, a very tough guy who insisted all his offspring be tough. She had four older brothers who taught her how to take some shit. That is to say, to take shit from *them*; if anyone else tried to give her a hard time, they taught her how to reverse the scene and send the trouble back from whence it came. If that didn't work, *wellllll*, the brothers could always clean up the slop.

"This is a real simple plan, guys," said Esmerelda. "You gotta bug out of town, right, Tim?"

"Sure do."

"Well, let's do this. Tomorrow, we all have a real good breakfast. Me, you, and Danny-boy go over to your place, and while you're getting shit together and writing that cheque, me and Danny-boy will show your stepdad the error of his ways. Perhaps instill in him the necessity of imploring God for guidance."

"Okay, I'll go up and pack up some clothes and shit, maybe grab some food, too."

"Tim, I'm pretty sure they sell food in America. Travel light—don't weigh yourself down with cans of soup or beans or nothing. So, we do that, then me and you go to the bank, then the streetcar down to the bus station, and get your skinny little ass across the border."

"But he'll call the cops as soon as we leave," Tim said.

"Well, that's where Danny-boy comes in. He can babysit your evil stepfather for a few hours. Your stepfather drinks and smokes a lot, right?"

Tim harrumphed in the affirmative.

"Then he and Danny-boy will get along just fine."

Tim finally had to ask. "So if I get into the States and am cool, what about you guys? They'll find out who you are. I don't want you guys going to jail."

Esmerelda leaned back and cracked her knuckles loudly over her head.

"It's like this, Tim. We're kinda pros at this kind of misbehaving. You know how psychotics and schizophrenics tend to have hallucinations?"

"I've heard," said Tim, while Danny nodded.

"Well, there are your standard hallucinations, ya know. You see shit, you hear shit. Just freaks your own self out, really. But there are these other things they call 'command hallucinations.' Those are the ones where something or someone in your brain tells you to do something..." Esmerelda lifted her arms up in a questioning pose. "So, worst thing is they send us back here. Or up onto a locked ward. Same thing, who cares? Right is right, there's a time when all humans need to do what's right, Timmy-boy. Don't you think?"

"I do think."

. . .

That night Tim had a hard time falling asleep. When he finally did, there was a dream of Marbea. She was in her yellow dress, of course, yellow ribbons in her yellow hair. They were lazing by the railroad tracks in the twilight, lightning bugs everywhere. They began to make love, somehow floating their way up onto the middle of the tracks, Tim on top, though neither seemed to be moving. A southbound train loaded with coal arrived from nowhere. It blew right on by, right over them. When it had passed, Marbea lay peaceful in yellow between the tracks as though in a dream herself. Tim was on the back of the coal train, waving goodbye. As if he were going into a tunnel: goodbye to her, this; then, to it all.

Lighthouse
Aayushi Jain

1

Bedtime is my favourite part of the day. That's when Mum comes to kiss me goodnight, always exactly on the middle of my forehead. She bends down. Her hair falls around my face, enclosing me like the leaves of a willow tree. Soft light filters through the strands. I close my eyes and let her leaves brush my cheek.

One morning, before school, I ask why she kisses me there.

"It's your third eye," she says, braiding my hair. "When I kiss it, it opens."

I think about this throughout the day. At night, after she leaves my room, I reach up from under the covers and carefully touch my forehead, feeling for eyelashes.

I wish my third eye could help me sleep. My parents close their bedroom door and lower their voices, but Mum always gets louder until she is shouting. She is wind slapping against the side of my face. Dad never shouts, but he is the deep rumbling earth that makes me grip the bedsheets. I count teddy bears on the wallpaper until I fall asleep.

2

I'm sleeping. I know I'm sleeping but I can't wake up. I am a spider trying to climb my cobweb up to the moon, but the sea won't let me. One by one, it cuts off my legs, but they keep growing back so I keep climbing. The moon smiles down and the sea glares up and my legs fall, again and again, into the dark water, like burnt matchsticks.

When the dream finally ends, I roll out of bed and creep across the landing to my parents' room. They are sleeping with their backs to each other. The gap separating them is wide enough for thousands of me. Like a river, I carve myself into the valley between their bodies and fall asleep.

3

It's Saturday and I am wearing billowing harem pants that smell like India, like red clay and fresh lotuses in monsoon season. Dad is out running errands, and Mum sits in the chaise, reading Kamala Markandaya's *Nectar in a Sieve*. I run around the house pretending to be a genie, granting wishes to potted ficuses and Grandma's blue china. I run past Mum, ask what her wish is, and she catches me by my waist, pulling me close.

"You," she whispers. I sink into her arms. She smells like sandalwood. *I am a tiny, happy genie. She is the warm lamp I curl into at night.*

4

Dad is in the living room. The TV is on and so is his phone screen, but he isn't looking at either. The knots above his eyebrows bulge, deepening the lines across his forehead. I stare at them. His forehead is a wrinkled carpet I can never pull straight.

Tonight, when they fight, they forget to close the door. I cover my ears but I can still hear them.

Wind stings my cheek. "I'm leaving!" it screams.

My third eye trembles and pulses out a warning.

5

On Sunday, Mum takes me swimming. She swims in the adult lanes and I play at the shallow end by the steps. My arm bands are yellow and see-through; when I look through them, everything changes. Suddenly I feel sad, without knowing why. I hold my breath, slip under the surface, and watch her through the water. She glows like a jellyfish, swimming toward and away. The water cradles me in its blue swinging belly.

6

Today in History we learn about the Greek gods. Poseidon is my favourite. We make posters, and Miss Arnold stands behind me to ask why I've drawn everyone with three eyes. Her face is scrunched up like a dried leaf.

"Make your pictures realistic." She hands me a dirty pink eraser.

I wonder if anyone has ever kissed her forehead. On the bus ride home, I draw everyone's third eye back in.

Mum doesn't answer the doorbell, so I get out my spare key. I find her in the guest bedroom, lying awake. I ask if she knows about Poseidon. She smiles, her eyes still and wet.

7

It's evening and Mum is still upstairs. She is on the phone to Grandma. Dad and I have microwave macaroni for dinner.

"Why is Mum talking to Grandma?"

"She isn't feeling well."

"Will she still come kiss me goodnight?"

His fork scratches the plate.

"Why isn't she feeling well?"

"She just needs someone to talk to."

"Can't she talk to you?"

His eyes go to the floor and he turns away. He is looking out the kitchen window, but it is completely dark outside.

8

I lie awake, listening for Mum's footsteps. When she finally comes, I pretend to be asleep. She brushes hair from my face; her cool lips feel like moonlight against my forehead. I keep my eyes closed, but as she walks away they snap open, searching for her in the dark. She stands in the doorway looking back, with an expression I haven't seen before.

That night I dream I am on a boat in the ocean, staring up. The eye on my forehead is wide open, refusing to blink. The moon is bright as it swings above from left to right, to left, to right… It is a hypnotist's watch dangling from the sky.

9

Dad opens the door when I come home from school. I follow him to the kitchen and watch him take macaroni from the freezer.

"Where's Mum?"

"At Grandma and Grandpa's."

"Can we go?"

He shakes his head. He is smiling the same way he smiles at strangers.

"Is she bringing back dessert?

"She's going to stay there."

He stares at the floor.

"For how long?"

His hands grip the edge of the kitchen counter. His smile shakes. It collapses and reconstructs itself.

"When is she coming back?"

His face twitches. "I don't know."

There is something stuck in his throat, and I realize it is sadness. I press myself into his body. He doesn't cry but I feel his chest heaving like an ocean.

10

I climb into bed with Dad and lie still. As I start to fall asleep, I think I hear her footsteps on the stairs, but it is just the dishwasher rumbling.

I reach my hand from under the covers and bring a fingertip to my lips. I kiss it silently and touch it to the middle of my forehead. I can feel my third eye, wet and blinking in the dark like a lighthouse. *I am a lighthouse. She is the spinning ship I search for at night.*

Quebec

ELECTRICALS USED & NEW. YOUR APPLIANCES FOR CASH. IN SHOP REPAIRS.
Lars Horn

On the table in front of you, the guts of a radio slump beside a blown-out television set. Seated across the table, the electrician unscrews the back panel on your radio alarm clock: "Stellar radiation, thunderstorms, echolocation, all got a pulse, right down to your household electricals"—the repairman taps your radio with the screwdriver—"slice through the Earth—air, sea, outer crust to molten core—and it'd be thrumming with frequencies."

The repairman readjusts his glasses, steel-rimmed, finely flecked with paint. "Nothing much here, just a loose connection on the circuit board. I can fix that now." The repairman stands, takes a soldering iron from a shelf behind him. The check of his shirt pulls taut over his back.

"Anyway, I'd always thought of radios and televisions as having a kind of pulse. I mean, I work in electricals, spend most of my time tuning the damn things, so that wasn't so new—frequency bands vibrating at different rates. Even the idea of naturally occurring frequencies—lightning discharges, that kind of thing—I'd read a bit on that, nothing extensive, mind, but again, you need a rough idea for the job. I went on a training course once: Radio Transmission for the Amateur Enthusiast. It dealt with how atmospheric conditions affect radio waves. That's when I first heard about the Earth's atmosphere having a pulse—Schumann resonance—named after some German scientist, I think. Anyhow, pretty clever guy, predicted that lightning discharges would create low-frequency pulsations in the cavity between the surface and the upper atmosphere of the Earth."

The repairman rummages in a drawer, removes a spool of solder.

"Thing is, and that's what I was reading about, the Earth's atmosphere pulses at the exact same rate as the human body. Scientists were doing brain scans, measuring the electrical impulses of the nervous system, and that's when they realized, turns out we're in sync with the Earth's atmospheric cavity."

You look around the room. Fluorescent tags explode pink, green, yellow on the screens of television sets: *SONY 4K HDR. SUPREME BRIGHTNESS, STUNNING REALISM.* In one corner, a light-bulb display board—some five feet high—hangs against the wall. You walk over to it.

Mounted into sockets in rows of five, light bulbs protrude from the chipboard. *ARBITRARY, GLOBE, BLOWN TUBULAR, CANDLE, BULGED REFLECTOR.* Below each bulb is a metal switch. Near the bottom of the board, the bulbs change from bright white to multi-coloured, the final rows a staccato of textured glass, candle twists.

"They think it might affect our internal clocks, hormonal secretion, sleep patterns—things like that."

In a bulb labelled *DARKROOM SAFE*, a three-spine stickleback twitches against the glass.

You look back at the repairman. He blows on the solder to make sure it's set. Sliding the circuit board back into the radio, he screws closed the plastic base, resets the time and date: "There, all linked up again." The repairman turns the radio round to face you: *[15:34]*. "They've even linked the frequencies with bodily states—behaviours, feelings—mapped out the whole spectrum right from the highest frequencies, when we're most awake, to the lowest, when we're unconscious or in deep, dreamless sleep."

You turn back to the display board, flick the metal switch beneath the darkroom safe lamp. The bulb glows red. The stickleback recoils from the filament. You click off the light. You turn to the repairman: "And disturbed sleep, what frequency is that?"

New Brunswick

The Country Vet
Charlie Fiset

The vet turned off the highway at a rotting hay bale that had arms and legs and a big red grin. It was cradling a sign that said *EGGS*. No chickens that she could see. The vet caught sight of the stallion in the pen with the run-in shed, same as when she visited yesterday, hay belly a little rounder. The stallion looked unhandled, tangle of red mane reaching down to his shoulder in burr-filled sheaves, legs thick with mud. The vet had been working the auction where he'd sold, the first auction she'd ever worked. Meat-buyers from the dog-food companies sat in the front row—grinning men in cowboy hats. A lame or wild horse couldn't go in the ring, so her job had been to cure a lot of equine "headaches" with bute. It'd been her last auction, too. She remembered thinking the wild brute devil would bring heaps of trouble to whoever fell for his pretty face, and that had turned out true, but not in the way she thought. She assumed he'd jumped the fence, and that's why the pony mare was in foal. But it turned out the owners had wanted to breed the mare—had done so willingly, even though anyone with any horse sense or even any common sense at all could tell she was far too small.

As the vet got out of her truck, the stallion bucked and kicked the fence, sending a shower of wood splinters flying from his cracked heels; a sliver hit her cheek. The yard dredged up a feeling of disgust in her, subtle, like the memory of a scent. It was a solitary little kingdom, one of the many peculiar bailiwicks of Timiskaming. The county was quilted together by old Dutch farming families who'd sold off most of their land to a conglomerate from down south.

The property was extravagance and decrepitude. The barn was new and huge, and so was the farmhouse, but the yard itself was a mess of rusted machinery: a smashed satellite dish, doorless fridges, piles of tires five feet high. It was all fenced in by a newly painted livestock fence, white and gleaming in the high noon sun. But the gates were electrified chain-link, with barbed metal on top.

The vet picked her way through the mess, heading to the barn and finding it empty. She checked the paddocks, but the pony mare was nowhere in sight. The vet was pissed. All she'd asked was that the mare be kept in until she'd had another look—but the locals were as likely to follow her directions as not. Maybe they'd turned her out, and she'd wandered far afield and foundered. The vet cursed as she headed up to the farmhouse, preparing for another long afternoon.

The memory of the pony mare's foal returned to her while she waited at the door. She'd left yesterday evening without speaking to the owners, because it had been so late, and because the vet had been in no state to see anyone. She knew it would be difficult to explain what she'd had to do to save the mare. The foal's head was too big to fit through the birth canal. The mare needed emergency surgery; no time to ship her to a clinic, and no clinic to ship to. The vet had given the owners a choice: the mare or the foal. They'd chosen the mare—their daughter's pony. The foal's body had been sleek and strong in the dark when she found his delicate nape, and slid the cutting wire into place. The mare jerked, tried to stand under heavy anaesthetic. The vet had quieted her. They'd waited too long—all of them always waited too damn long to call for help. *Let nature take its course* was their motto. She'd saved the mare, anyway.

The door was answered by the woman she'd seen the day before. Again, the vet had the impression that the woman was in pain, someone who had been trapped indoors for a long time, heaped in by a nest of broken, rusted metal.

"And how did the mare do?" the vet asked, averting her eyes from the sick woman. "I'd like to have another look at her, if you don't mind."

The woman said something the vet didn't hear, a cough and a mumble. No, she couldn't see the pony mare.

The vet wasn't taken aback. Most locals didn't believe in follow-ups. "It'll only take a moment. Free of charge, of course. It's for my own peace of mind."

Through her haze, the woman looked almost troubled. "When my daughter checked on her pony this morning, she was moping around with her head down, not eating, just miserable, like she couldn't understand what had happened to her baby. So my husband brought her out back."

At first the vet didn't think she'd understood.

The woman was fumbling in her handbag for her chequebook. "She looked so sad," she said. "I just couldn't stand to look at her."

The vet watched the stallion in her rear-view mirror as she started back up the long drive. He was pawing at the hay strewn about his corral, drowning the fresh green strands in the mud.

Working in the north, she told herself, was still better than the work she'd get at a hatchery or racetrack or auction house down south. Here, at least her work was personal. She was her own boss. All she needed was her truck, which she sometimes even slept in.

Most of the time, she loved the adventure of her life and sometimes she even felt like she was making a difference. Most of the time, she tried to focus on what good she could do, though occasionally she wondered if there was any good she really could do. I saved a life yesterday, she reminded herself. In the silence of the cab she said, *I save lives.*

Prince Edward Island

Three Poems
Kandace Hagen

Oy Gevalt

My lover is white
sometimes.
My lover is white
until they're not.

Until.

A silver wolf
with an assault rifle
decides otherwise.

Men don't carry
pistols in Canada
but culture bleeds
over borders
into houses
of assembly.

The holocaust.

The war that
eclipsed the sun
and we good
gentiles thought
we were grown now.

Judah Samet
war camp survivor
four minutes late
to the Tree of Life
witnessed his faith
gunned down
eleven times
on holy ground
bore witness
to a rebirth
of hate.

Tell me how did we not see
tell me how we missed this
inevitability.

When my lover's
whiteness
becomes paltry
I want you to tell me
how we've grown.

No, don't tell me
go tell them

how we've grown
how we've learned.

Tell them

mir 're nebekhdik
we're sorry.

Cattle Lists

I have been a catalyst,
by which I mean
it was my responsibility
to record each and every
chattel alphabetically
in a ledger for my proprietor
who was seated
at the right hand of the father.

I have been a catalyst,
the cause of one more round,
the reason you stumbled home
at 5:00 a.m. into the seething arms
of a man who doubted your sincerity,
that you and I were only friends.

I have been a catalyst,
by which I mean
the livestock followed me
around Eden's pasture as if
I were an anointed mother,
until lightning cracked the sky
and mobs of sheep
and sounders of pigs
took safe haven in the orchard
under the apple trees, a foreshadowing
of my unholiest departure
from the sweet groves of Eden.

I have been a catalyst,
the cause of sleepless anguish
and holes punched into walls.
"I promise, that was the last time,"
never true when spoken from
my mouth, a mouth that craved
sacred water trapped in canals,
the lewdness of lavender pressed
between spread willing lips,
and the milk from the blessed mother
to suckle me gently into womanhood,
awakening unquenchable thirst.

I was a mighty catalyst
who made cattle lists
until the dyke broke
and the holy waters ran free.

My Ravine

This year my ravine
is boreal and withdrawn.
The earth cannot thaw
the sleeping children
tucked deeply into the bones
of the ground.

Former lovers left notes
restrained beneath stone
and traced outlines of my bare feet
in the stark, hardened soil.

In my ravine, where I preserve
all my good intentions
and the wind is hell-bent
and the saplings cannot take root

swarms of elderly women
in slickers and plastic hairnets
try to find warmth
while forgetting all their
worst intentions.

In my ravine, where I
keep everything and nothing
and the trees do not hold
on to their leaves.

My breasts shrivel with frostbite
and the women with husbands
I never knew but hate howbeit
gather in hordes
to plant cicadas
in the frozen earth.

Nova Scotia

Also Like Life
Ryan Paterson

"What exactly are you looking at?" Her lips tighten into a smile and she presses her back against the theatre's fog-painted door.

"You all set?" he says.

This happens a lot, he gets caught staring and loses track, has to scramble by answering her question with an unrelated one.

"I'm right here," she says, "inviting you to join me out in the marvellous world."

She tiptoes outside and her red trench coat flares up under the marquee. He catches the door and stumbles onto the sidewalk. The rain has stopped, but a canopy of clouds shuts out the moon. Tonight belongs to the traffic lights and illuminated signs of Quinpool Road. Gasps of steam spill out of the propped-open doors of takeout joints. Puddles glisten like stars in an asphalt galaxy.

She takes his hand, their fingers nest together.

"Just until the light changes, okay?" she says. "I promise to let go."

Her grip tightens. She knows this is harder for him than it should be.

"Did you like the movie?" she asks. They are always his movies, but she always goes along with him. For her, it isn't about the screen. She just wants to be with him in the dark, their shadows cast into a sea of silhouettes.

"Yeah," he says. "It was great."

"What'd you like about it?"

He searches one end of the street to its vanishing point and then the other. He's seen a lot of movies, but still finds it hard to talk about them. Only hours later, or sometimes days, can he assemble the pieces.

"I mean, visually it was stunning," he says. "And the performances were great."

It isn't working. He goes back to the question again.

"Did you like it?"

"It was fine," she says. "But all your movies are so sad. Either the couple never gets together, or they do and it doesn't work out. Sometimes they just up and die."

"Real life is like that, too, you know."

"Ah, yes. There's the old philosophizing. I was starting to worry."

The truth is he really didn't have anything to say about the movie yet. Right now, all he can think about is the moment when he put his hand on her thigh in the dark and she held it there and leaned in on his shoulder. It was a kind of flash. For one second, he thought he could understand her—this desire she had to be tethered to another person. He felt it for maybe the first time.

Orange gives way to white, and her fingers abandon his. She lets go and runs into the crosswalk but stops halfway, right in the middle of the street. Like a kid, she squats down low, knees almost at her shoulders, then she pushes off again and jumps, really jumps, dead centre into a massive puddle. Beads of red light shoot up on all sides of her. He watches from the curb, trying to take it all in: the glow of her jacket under the traffic light, the shallow pools of rainwater and humidity-blurred storefront signs. Then she's gone again, running to the other side of the street. It all carries this sensation of heightened reality, as if he is watching it, as if all of this is up there on the big screen.

"Will you come on!" she shouts, and her finger points up at the flashing hand. There is always a countdown. He hadn't noticed this before.

Four.

Three.

Two.

He has to go. He bursts forth into the haze of light, darts across the street and makes it to the other side. He wraps his arms around her waist, lifts her off the ground, and spins her around. She kicks out at the thick air. It really is something you've seen before.

They release and he takes off, running up Oxford Street, she in pursuit. She reaches the end of the block, but he's already on the other side, hands pressed against his thighs, breathing hard.

"Wait for me!" she squeals.

"No!"

Wind rolls in and the leaves overhead shudder all at once. Rain fires down, so heavy and dense, it seems to fall in pillars.

"We've got to go!"

She catches up and snatches his hand as she passes. He stays in step with her, his own feet drowned out by the machine-gun chatter of raindrops and the slap of her boots on the wet sidewalk.

At home, shirts are stripped off in one go, but jeans have to be grappled with, shuffled down inch by inch. Even then, their slick bodies shine in the dull light. He presses close to her against the bathroom radiator, trying to reach the towels on the back of the door. He's still breathing hard, his chest rising and falling against her back. Up close, he sees that artery in her neck jumping in rhythm with his breath.

Wet clothes are hung wherever there's room: the radiator, the shower rod, the doorknob. Her towel hits the tile and she scurries for the bedroom. He follows her through the apartment, catching glimpses of her as she moves from kitchen to living room to bedroom. He finds her smothered in a cocoon of blankets, framed by the doorway.

"Want something hot?" he asks. "Coffee or tea—"

"Tea, please."

He fills the kettle with cold water, puts it on, and sits down naked at the kitchen table. His balls tighten against the chair's cool veneer. The water is slow to heat at first, barely whispering, like it's just not going to happen tonight. Only once he's settled in—once his chest has stopped pounding—does the kettle peak fast, screaming and rattling against the element.

He walks a tightrope to the bedroom, a mug in each hand. He's still drunk on it all—the heat, rain, light. His hand on her thigh. Her cheek on his shoulder. He opens his mouth to tell her what it means, but it's too late. She's gone off into another space—eyes closed, hair splayed on the pillow, mouth agape. Drool. She lies on her side, hands tucked under her damp hair, the sheet on his side of the bed overturned, inviting him to join her.

Rain keeps time on the bedroom window, only the ghost of a street light for a view. The windows across the street a sequence of empty screens. Some things can be seen in a dark room, but not tonight. He leaves the mugs to cool on the dresser, finds his place in bed, wraps his arms around her waist, and pulls her close. His thighs meet hers, her back warms his chest. He looks at the nape of her still neck and closes his eyes.

Life and Limb
Beth Hitchcock

I got a dollhouse for Christmas the year I turned eight. Putting it together was a group effort that kept my parents, grandparents, and aunt occupied until two in the morning: Every tiny piece of furniture had to be unwrapped and assembled, each tin of thimble-sized food placed in the kitchen cabinets. The process involved equal parts cursing and gin consumption. When they finished, the perfect dollhouse family—a mother and father, son and daughter—sat around a plug-in fireplace that glowed as brightly as the four-volt electrical system would allow. It was my first dream house that wasn't our own.

Something was wrong with Dad. The toes on his left leg had turned a garish shade of purple around Christmastime; now, in March, they were black. I heard Mom whispering, "vascular disease" and "gang green" on the phone to her sister. That night, I lay board-stiff and sleepless in my bed. I knew it was only a matter of time until the green gang came to take Dad away. Imagine my surprise to find them in blue—two broad-shouldered men putting Dad on a stretcher. As the ambulance pulled away and Mom talked with the neighbours, I crawled into the front-hall closet and crouched beneath the coats.

Mom, a perfectionist, had wallpapered the closet's interior to match the foyer. In the dark, I stroked the paper, soothed by the sensation of my fingers darting over its flocked damask pattern, which gave way to smooth, shiny silver sections in relief. I touched the paper in the same spot until it split at the seam.

After emerging to find a pencil, I stole back to the closet and slid the plywood bi-fold door along its track. Safely back inside, I breathed in the scent of rubber tinged with mothballs and swatted away the teeth of long zippers gnawing at my leg.

Beth is scared

I wrote on the plaster where the paper, coaxed by my anxious fingertips, had curled up. Calm enveloped me like a cape.

While Dad was in the hospital, Mom bought me a book of Victorian dollhouse wallpaper, elaborate small-scale patterns that were fussier than the dollhouse's mid-century modern style. Undeterred, I decided the dollhouse needed a fresh new look. *Makeover Madness!*—it was a line I'd seen on the cover of one of Mom's magazines.

I cut out the pieces and fit them to the walls, the way I'd seen her do. Matching the seams tried my patience, so I threw a large piece on the living room floor in frustration. Mom was too distracted to notice that it stayed there for several weeks. "Don't mind the mess, I'm re-wallpapering," I'd say to friends, affecting the world-weary voice of a grown-up whose decorator won't return calls.

The doctors sent Dad home without half of two of his toes, but soon his foot grew numb again. I'd pull off the left sock at night while he watched TV so I could inspect it.

"Doesn't look too good, does it, sweetie?" The skin was marbled with purple blotches that crawled up his leg, a rotting banana of a limb. "They say I might need another operation."

My behind-the-wallpaper prayers increased in frequency and fervency. I'd pulled back a large flap, making room for each pencil scratch:

Beth promises to be good
Beth will clean her room
Beth hopes her dad doesn't die

Dad went back to the hospital, but this time we dropped

him off with a suitcase. At home, Mom was making a lot of phone calls again, and whispering new words: "blockage"... "amputation"..."prosthesis."

"What's amputation?" I asked her later, as we drove to the hospital for a pre-op visit.

"Daddy's leg isn't getting the blood it needs," she said. "The doctors have to remove part of it so he can feel better."

I slept with Mom that night, curled up in Dad's divot on the king-sized mattress.

When we visited post-surgery, Dad's legs were hidden under blankets and I could almost pretend nothing had happened—except he didn't know me. Dad had lost my name, stuttering and staring past me with panicked eyes. "Don't worry," Mom said, her hand on my shoulder. "It's because of the painkillers. Daddy's just confused." That night, I ripped an entire panel of wallpaper from the closet.

When Dad came home, he wore pyjamas all day and watched TV. No longer filled out, the left pant leg flapped, so Mom made a makeshift hem with safety pins. Sometimes at night, the *click-hop-shuffle-click* of his walker woke me up when he made his way to the bathroom. Other times it was the moans—phantom pains for a leg no longer there.

Soon I returned to my dollhouse-redecorating job. As I pulled the family out of their respective bedrooms, I took a closer look at their poreless plastic bodies. The mother's no-nonsense bob struck me as an affront: too shiny, too sleek, too unruffled by reality. I took out my craft scissors and, through sobs, hacked her hair into an unflattering shag.

Next, I popped off the dollhouse dad's left leg.

Even with one big plastic black shoe on his right foot, the dad couldn't stand. He'd forever be off balance. I positioned the dollhouse mother and daughter on either side. Together, they propped him up.

Newfoundland

Woolly Adelgid
Amy Donovan

The two-hour drive from Spryfield to Kejimkujik begins in dreamy silence. Louise is trying to fight her way through Lévi-Strauss's *Savage Mind* even though Theory 2 and the windowless classroom in the leering brutalist building seem worlds, not provinces, away.

They push southwest on the 103—her least favourite highway in Nova Scotia, a never-ending no-place of one-way through rock cut. She thinks about how Ben is more in tune than your average dude with what the old anthropologist called *savage thought*—*savage* for him meaning *untamed*. Something less mediated, more animal about Benny. This the reason she flew here to talk in person, among trees. This the reason she fell in love with him to begin with, and kept fighting. To all her friends: *We're not that different. We care about the same things, just he cares with his guts and his heart.*

Louise cares *about* his guts and his heart. All the juicy parts of him now closed to her.

Ben's voice displaces the quiet like honey sliding into water. His down-home accent, words always warmly furred, the tone of voice she recognizes as belonging to people he cares about when he isn't in a state of mind to care about himself. "I got myself feeling angry all the time," he says. "I'm not connected."

It's not a surprise, but not an emotion she associates with the Benny she knows. "What is it you're angry about?" His truck's grumble makes her loud.

His list covers the remainder of the drive, off the highway and through tiny Caledonia, its meagre rows of just-better-than-ramshackle bungalows and almost-saltboxes, not that you'd call them that in this place of leafy trees and fairy-blue lakes. His list outlasts the Parks Canada road, suddenly free of potholes; sweeps them past the shit-brown entry kiosk, hunter's-orange bath towel draped over the window; sputters, finally, and loses steam when he cuts the engine at the pylons by the gate. Pylons and gate the same industrial orange, like humanity shouting.

Louise is glad to get past the orange; feels a little more air in the air once they begin hiking along the access road. Closed for snowshoeing and it's the middle of January, but there's only a dusting of snow on ice, lit lead-white under the cold sun fingering through the evergreens.

A couple of kilometres in, pithy white spruce morph into gods: the boundary line where the hemlocks start. They stand for a moment, cowed. Then Benny says: "Thinking about that bug makes me sick." His voice splinters. She thinks: *Here it comes.*

"I know." For years the pride of Kejie was that the hemlock bug *wasn't* here.

What does it mean to rest your identity on an absence?

Ben crouches beside a fallen hemlock. The jagged fault line between the stump and the prostrate trunk is dotted with honeycomb-like holes. A thousand of them, a million. The spongy wood sand-hued with overtones of wet viridian, webbed along its scraggly edges. "Did the bug do that?" Louise asks.

Benny can look at a twisted trunk and tell you about the prevailing wind patterns it's experienced. He can touch a living trunk and say if it is dead inside.

"No," he says. "Ants. Unlucky, or waiting to be weeded out... You know how indigenous people say animals give themselves to hunters?"

"Yes." Louise's throat is clogged, suddenly, with tiny scurrying ants.

"I've been wondering," Ben says, gesturing to the honeycombed hemlock guts. "Who's doing the giving here?

You'd think the tree, but I'm not sure the ants aren't making decisions, too. Giving the tree *away*, to the forest. Seems to me like more than a two-way operation."

Louise nods. "A collective mind." Her ants break through some kind of membrane, begin moving along neural passageways.

They keep walking. Eventually Ben says, "What do you think our current relationship status is?"

"Fucked." Then: "What do you think?"

"I'm not here."

Benny sits her down on another fallen hemlock to cry. He's brought a giant Dairy Milk bar but no Kleenex. She blows her nose on half-frozen oak and maple leaves prised from mossy hummocks. "Just do a snot rocket," says Ben, and tries to teach her how. "Hold your nose *upright*," he keeps saying. "*Lean* out."

Over and over she fails, and finally they burst into laughter, her nose still thickly stuffed—maybe that's ants, too. Something awakens around them that does not come from her or from Ben. A gift of the hemlocks, perhaps, or the moss. Something lifts away from her; the writhing colony inside her goes still.

"Thank you for coming here," says Benny. "I couldn't have been kind, in the city."

You lose something, Louise's supervisor had told her, with the English translation of *Savage Mind*, because half the book's point rests on the French title: *Pensée Sauvage*. It means *savage thought*, but also *wild pansy*.

The joke—and the point—is: pansies are domesticated.

They walk along the frozen lake to return to the truck. The ice is yellow under late-day sun, everything backlit like shadow puppets: Ben leaning out over the ice, one hand clutching a thick branch, the other reaching (toward what?). His long hair glinting, all of him framed by an archway of spindly, naked tamarack and feathered pine. This beautiful body that will never be hers again, the shape of it simultaneously turning her on and making her nauseous.

Deeper in her churning midsection, rhizomes of something like gratitude make themselves known. Growing outward, poking at some organ she probably couldn't name. Yes: she is *grateful* to Ben, as if he were part of the forest itself. Invisible woolly adelgids be damned. Invisible woolly adelgids, *try me*.

Between the path and the shoreline, meltwater from a days-ago flood has pooled into foggy ice. Rangy black spruce trunks stretch out of it like frail, grasping fingers. Benny's shoulders have fallen out of the hunch he was wearing in the truck. The ice gleams like metal under the sun.

Louise wonders if they are still called *vernal pools* when the water is frozen, and it isn't yet spring.

About the Authors

Miles Steyn was born in KwaZulu-Natal, South Africa, moved to Vancouver at age nine, and has been back and forth ever since. He is a graduate of the Creative Writing MFA Program at the University of Victoria, and his work has appeared in publications across Canada. In 2015, Miles's essay "Wire to the Sky" was shortlisted for *EVENT Magazine's* creative nonfiction contest. In 2018, he was long-listed for the CBC Nonfiction Prize. In 2019, he was selected as one of five emerging writers to participate in the RBC Charles Taylor Mentorship Program. Miles is currently exploring themes of nationality, loss, and difference in his first memoir, *Shongololo Pie*.

Conor Kerr is a Metis writer from Amiskwaciy Waskahegan by way of Buffalo Pound Lake. He works at the Indigenous Student Services Centre at NorQuest College and is a student in UBC's MFA program. Conor is a proud listener, storyteller, harvester, and Labrador retriever enthusiast.

Matthew James Weigel is a poet and artist creating in Treaty 6 territory. He is of Dene, Metis, British, and German ancestry and holds a Bachelor of Science in Biological Sciences from the University of Alberta. With a demonstrated passion for invertebrates, and special emphasis on sponges, Matthew James champions what goes most unnoticed. He continues to develop his poetics by exploring a variety of interfaces between water, land, air, people, writing, speaking, and material arts.

Kate Spencer was born in Moose Jaw, Saskatchewan, to a large and blended family. Like her family, now scattered all over Canada, she too travelled coast to coast before returning to the prairie. She is currently writing a Master's thesis on confession in James Joyce at the University of Regina. Kate is also pursuing poetry and home renovations.

Sarah Mintz is a graduate student in the English program at the University of Regina. Her creative writing thesis concerns Jewish identity and tradition mediated through popular culture. She holds degrees from both Concordia and McGill and spends her time reading, writing, working, and walking around.

Matthew Hay is a writer most days. Residing in Winnipeg, he can usually be found— Actually, he really ought not to be found. He's got writing to do and is all too accepting of distractions (especially if those distractions come bearing carrot cake). Matthew recently graduated from the University of Winnipeg.

Chloe Burrows Moore is a writer from Brampton, Ontario, who currently lives in Windsor with her husband and her cat, Gatsby. She has worked as a researcher, an editor for Black Moss Press, and an intern with Biblioasis. She has a degree in Creative Writing from the University of Windsor and has been published in several student literary periodicals.

Evelyna Ekoko-Kay is a queer poet and activist of black-mixed heritage from Hamilton, Ontario. She is an MFA candidate at the University of Guelph, as well as a Real Nuisance. Her writing has been featured in *Tenderness Lit*, *Voicemail Poems*, *Pineapples Against Patriarchy Zine*, *The Undergraduate Review*, and *Collective Reflections*.

David Dupont's work has been shortlisted for the CBC Short Story Prize. He's currently completing a degree in Creative Writing at York University, where he has been awarded for his short fiction. He lives in Toronto.

Laura Goslinski is a writer who is double-majoring in Mental Health Studies and English at the University of Toronto Scarborough. She is also very tall.

Natalia Orasanin is a writer in Toronto currently completing her undergraduate degree at Ryerson University. Her writing explores fragmented memories, reoccurring dreams, and the landscapes that shape us. Her interests include poetry, short fiction, film, and illustration.

A retired typographer, **Colin Buchanan** grew up in various towns and cities in Ontario. He spent a decade living in the American Deep South, listening to songs and acquiring stories. A recent graduate of the Humber School for Writers, he lives in Toronto. His contribution is drawn from his unpublished first novel, *Yellow Women's Doorbells*.

Aayushi Jain is an English literature student from the UK and has just completed a year-long exchange program at Ottawa's Carleton University. She enjoys writing poetry and short stories, and also performs her original songs at local venues. Her work traverses the boundary between prose and poetry, using an intimate framework of recurring imagery to create quiet, dreamlike narratives.

Lars Horn lives in Montreal.

Charlie Fiset is from northern Ontario. She completed an MA in Creative Writing from the University of New Brunswick. Her work has twice appeared in *The Journey Prize Anthology*, was a runner-up for PEN Canada's New Voices award, and was longlisted for the Commonwealth Prize. She recently finished her first novel.

Kandace Hagen is a fledgling poet, ramshackle lesbian, and impromptu feminist who draws her inspiration from the grit in the air and salt in the water of Prince Edward Island.

Ryan Paterson is a writer from Halifax.

Beth Hitchcock has an MFA in Creative Nonfiction from the University of King's College and is the former editor-in-chief of *Canadian House & Home* magazine. She lives in Toronto.

Amy Donovan holds a master's in creative writing from Memorial University. Her work has appeared in *Riddle Fence, Newfoundland Quarterly,* and *Best Kind,* an anthology of Newfoundland creative nonfiction. She is currently pursuing a PhD in anthropology at McGill University, where her research focuses on more-than-human storytelling and the social lives of whales. She is from Cape Breton, Nova Scotia.

About the Mentors

The unsung heroes (who are about to be sung a little) of this collection are the mentors of the emerging writers featured in this anthology. The mentors hail from some of the academic institutions across this country that have creative writing programs. Many are writers themselves, very accomplished ones. They have not only helped select some of the most promising writers they have discovered and helped to bring along, but have also worked with them on the pieces featured here to make them as good as they can be. They, too, deserve credit and applause.

—Joseph Kertes and Geoffrey Taylor

David Leach is a professor of creative nonfiction in the Department of Writing at the University of Victoria and the author of *Fatal Tide: When the Race of a Lifetime Goes Wrong* and *Chasing Utopia: The Future of the Kibbutz in a Divided Israel*. David's selection is by Miles Steyn.

Andrew Gray is the program coordinator at UBC Creative Writing and the author of two books: *Small Accidents* and *The Ghost Line*. Andrew's selection is by Conor Kerr.

Thomas Wharton teaches creative writing at the University of Alberta and is the author of three prize-winning books: *Icefields*, *Salamander*, and *The Logograph*. He has also written a YA fantasy trilogy and a history book for small children. Thomas's selection is by Matthew James Weigel.

Michael Trussler has published literary criticism, creative nonfiction, poetry, and short fiction, including *Encounters, Accidental Animals, A Homemade Life,* and *Light's Alibi*. Michael teaches creative writing at the University of Regina. Michael's selections are by Kate Spencer and Sarah Mintz.

Jonathan Ball teaches creative writing at the University of Winnipeg. He is the author of *Ex Machina, Clockfire, The Politics of Knives,* and *John Paizs's Crime Wave*. Jonathan's selection is by Matthew Hay.

Karl Jirgens, former Head of English at the University of Windsor, is author of four books of fiction and criticism. He is currently Chair of the Creative Writing program and a professor at University of Windsor. Karl's selection is by Chloe Burrows-Moore.

Catherine Bush is the author of four novels, including *The Rules of Engagement* (2000) and *Accusation* (2013), with a new novel forthcoming in 2020. She has been the Coordinator of the University of Guelph Creative Writing MFA, in Toronto, since 2008. Catherine's selection is by Evelyna Ekoko-Kay.

Michael Helm is the author of four novels, as well as personal essays and writings on fiction, poetry, and visual arts. He's an Associate Professor of English and Creative Writing at York University, and a Guggenheim Fellow. He lives in the Dundas Valley, in Ontario. Michael's selections are by David Dupont.

Andrew Westoll is the author of two books of literary nonfiction and a novel. He teaches Creative Writing and English at the University of Toronto Scarborough. Andrew's selection is by Laura Goslinski.

Dale Smith is a scholar and poet on the faculty of English at Ryerson University. His publications of poetry include *Slow Poetry in America* (2014) and *Sons* (2017), with *Shreve* forthcoming. Dale's selection is by Natalia Orasanin.

David Bezmozgis is a writer and filmmaker. His most recent book is *Immigrant City: Stories*. He is the director of the Humber School for Writers. David's selection is by Colin Buchanan.

Nadia Bozak is an Assistant Professor of English and the coordinator of the Creative Writing Concentration at Carleton University. She is the author of two novels, a collection of short stories, and a film theory monograph. **Richard Taylor** has taught writing at Carleton University since 1996. He has published a book of short stories, a novel, a memoir, *House Inside the Waves*, and is working on a book about swimming around the world with writers. Nadia and Richard's selection is by Aayushi Jain.

Kate Sterns is the co-ordinator of the creative writing program at Carleton University. She is the author of several radio plays and a novel, *Thinking About Magritte*. Kate's selection is by Lars Horn.

Mark Anthony Jarman teaches at the University of New Brunswick where he is a fiction editor with *The Fiddlehead*. He is the author of *Knife Party at the Hotel Europa, My White Planet, 19 Knives,* and the travel book *Ireland's Eye*. His *Selected Stories* is forthcoming from Biblioasis Press. Mark's selection is by Charlie Fiset.

Richard Lemm teaches creative writing and literature at the University of Prince Edward Island. He has published six poetry collections, most recently *Jeopardy*; a short fiction collection, *Shape of Things to Come*; and a biography, *Milton Acorn: In Love and Anger*. Richard's slections are by Kandace Hagen.

Alexander MacLeod is a fiction writer and an associate professor of English at Saint Mary's University in Halifax. He won a 2019 O. Henry Prize for his short story "Lagomorph," originally published in *Granta*. Alexander's selection is Ryan Paterson.

Kim Pittaway is the executive director of the MFA in Creative Nonfiction Program at the University of King's College in Halifax, Canada's only low-residency MFA devoted to the craft and business of nonfiction. Kim's selection is by Beth Hitchcock.

Robert Finley is the coordinator of Memorial University's Creative Writing Program. His publications include *The Accidental Indies, A Ragged Pen, K. L. Reich,* and Best Kind: New Writing Made in Newfoundland. He lives in St. John's. Robert's selection is by Amy Donovan.

Colophon

Manufactured as the first edition of
Write Across Canada: An Anthology of Emerging Writers
to celebrate the 40th anniversary of the
Toronto International Festival of Authors

Copy edited by Stuart Ross
Cover design by Gareth Lind / Lind Design
Text by Jay Millar

bookhugpress.ca